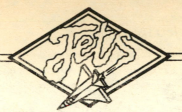

Monty, *the dog who wears glasses*

Colin West

Look out for more *Jets* from Collins

First published by A & C Black Ltd in 1989
Published by Collins in 1990
18 17 16
Collins is an imprint of HarperCollins*Publishers* Ltd,
77-85 Fulham Palace Road, Hammersmith, London W6 8JB

The HarperCollins website address is
www.fireandwater.com

ISBN 0 00 673681-5

The author and the illustrator assert the moral right to be
identified as the author and the illustrator of the work.
A CIP record for this title is available from the British Library.
Printed and bound in Great Britain by
Caledonian International Book Manufacturing Ltd, Glasgow

The Reason Why

This is Monty. He looks rather unusual.

I bet you're wondering why I'm wearing glasses.

MONTY

Well, one day, before Monty took to wearing glasses, he was taking young Simon Sprod for a walk. He was waiting for Simon outside the sweet shop, when he *almost* had a nasty accident.

A man on a bicycle swerved to avoid
Monty, and only *just* managed to
keep his balance.

Simon rushed out. The man looked over his shoulder as he rode off, and shouted:

What that dog needs is a pair of glasses!

That evening,
Simon thought more
about glasses.

Not that Monty was
short-sighted or anything, but
a pair of glasses might help to
remind him of his near-accident.
They might make him more careful
in future.

So Simon found an old pair of
sunglasses and took out both lenses.
Then he put them on Monty's nose.

Monty didn't like the glasses much.
They pinched his nose and felt
uncomfortable. So Simon loosened
the tiny screws in the hinges and
eased the ear-pieces wider apart.

That did it. They fitted perfectly.
Everyone agreed that Monty looked
even more handsome now.

But the new glasses didn't seem to cure his habit of accidents.

MONTY!
Mind that vase!

Monty's Barbecue

Mr and Mrs Sprod had visitors.
This was bad news for Monty, as
there were fewer chairs to go round.

Still, it wasn't *all* bad news.

The Sprods were good hosts. There was a lot of laughter and there was talk of a barbecue in the garden if the rain held off.

Monty loved barbecues more than anyone because they meant his favourite food –

He was soon on the patio.

'Look at Monty!' Mrs Jackson cried.
'Oh, he always does that in the nice
weather,' said Mrs Sprod.
'Shall we join him?' someone else
suggested.

Soon Mr Sprod had put on a frilly apron and taken charge of cooking the sausages.

Mrs Nutford was Monty's favourite visitor. She was a vegetarian, although she was too polite to refuse food that was given her.

But Monty didn't do so well with other people.

Another burnt offering!

Suddenly it started to rain and everyone ran back indoors.

How can they bear to leave their sausages?

At last Monty came in, dripping wet.

Monty at School

It was Monday morning and the Sprod children, Simon and Josie, were off to school.

That morning, Monty sneaked out of the back door and followed Simon and Josie down the street. No one took much notice of him, and he was able to follow them all the way.

Almost there!

Simon and Josie hurried into school.

Monty lost sight of them.

Which way did they go?

19

Monty took the first corridor.

Inside a large room, he found
some comfy chairs.

And soon
he was
fast asleep.

Monty was having a lovely dream
about a huge chocolate cake,
when he was woken by a very loud
electric bell.

RINNNGGG!

Soon the room was invaded by . . .

. . . lots of funny-looking grown-ups.

Then they all began trying to guess
where Monty had come from.
Some of them made a fuss of him,
while others were less friendly.

Then a little face peered round the door. It was Mary Worth from Class 1, and she'd come to the staffroom to hand in some lost property.

Of course she saw Monty sitting there. Soon the news was spreading around the playground.

Simon and Josie realized it could only be Monty. They went rather nervously to claim him.

Monty was glad to see some familiar faces.

Mrs Prendlethorpe, the headmistress, was glad to get the matter sorted out.

She made it plain that she didn't want Monty in school again.
But just this once, he was allowed to sit at the back of the classroom . . .

. . . and later to have some school
dinner . . .

. . . and then to join in a game of
rounders.

Mrs Prendlethorpe needn't have worried about Monty visiting again. Although he liked the comfy chair, he didn't care for the rest of the day's activities.

Monty at the Library

Josie was off to buy her mum a newspaper. She'd got some letters to post first, and Monty had the job of carrying them to the post box.

Everyone they passed was most
impressed, and Monty felt quite
proud.

Josie popped the letters into the box
and then bought the newspaper.
Monty carried it all the way home.

Everyone was just as impressed as before, and Mrs Sprod gave Monty a chocolate biscuit for being so helpful.

In the afternoon, Monty heard
Mrs Sprod reminding Simon to
return a library book which was due
back that day.
Simon would
have to pay a
fine if the book
was late.

Maybe this is my chance to earn another biscuit!

So when no one was looking, Monty took the book between his teeth and sneaked out of the house.

He made his way to the library.
People stopped to stare at him as he
went by.

A dog with glasses
carrying a book—
how novel!

At the corner of Tower Road,
there was a big puddle
on the pavement.
As Monty was edging his way round it . . .

. . . someone in a passing car hooted at him.

TOOT TOOT!

EEEEEKK!

And as Monty yelped in surprise . . .

PLOP!

the book fell into the muddy puddle.

Monty retrieved it and gave it a
good shake to dry it off.
But the pages were still a bit soggy.

Monty reached the library and
climbed the steps with the book
safe and sound. He presented it
eagerly to the lady behind the desk.

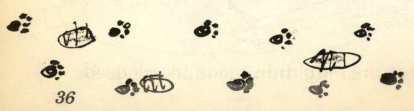

But the lady didn't look too pleased.

She took the book between finger and thumb, and looked at the damage.

Covered in mud.
Pages stuck together.
Deep teeth marks in cover.
Totally beyond repair!

Then she picked up a pen and wrote a note for Monty to take away.

Perhaps it's a thank-you note

Monty found Mrs Sprod in the
living room on her hands and knees.
He dropped the note in front of her.
'What's that?' asked Simon,
who was also on all fours.

Mrs Sprod looked at the note.
'It's from the library,' she said.
'It's about that book we've been
looking for all afternoon.'

Then she read aloud.

Monty didn't get another chocolate
biscuit that day.

Monty's Christmas

It was Christmas Eve.

Soon Father Christmas would be coming down the chimney.

'Who is Father Christmas, anyway?' Monty wondered.

When Simon and Josie were
in bed . . .

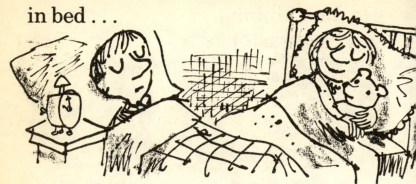

. . . and Mr and Mrs Sprod were
watching TV . . .

. . . Monty was
in his
basket in
the kitchen.

But he wasn't sleeping.

He was thinking.

Monty decided he'd help out.
He padded into the living room.

Monty sat down by the fireplace
under the coloured lights of the
Christmas tree. He waited for
Father Christmas to arrive.

He waited . . .

and waited . . .

and waited.

Suddenly, Monty was disturbed by someone walking round the room.

'That's funny,' he thought, as he opened one eye. 'The man's got a sack all right, but he hasn't got a big white beard.'

Monty leapt up and nipped the burglar on the ankle.

Then Mrs Sprod came down to
find out what was the matter.
She came into the living room and
switched on the light.

Monty got a big surprise.

The man with the sack was
Mr Sprod.

'I was just putting the presents
round the Christmas tree and that
daft dog attacked me!' he moaned,
still rubbing his ankle.

Monty was amazed. Mr Sprod, it seemed, was really Father Christmas.

Monty could have kicked himself –
he'd missed seeing Mr Sprod come
down the chimney.

How on earth
he finds time to
deliver everyone's
presents and work
at the office, I'll
never know!

Monty at the Supermarket

Mrs Sprod was at the entrance to the supermarket.

'I'll only be ten minutes,' Mrs Sprod told Monty, as she took a trolley from the line and went inside.

Monty hated waiting.
The supermarket looked so inviting.
He could see bright lights and people having trolley races.

After a few minutes, the man
in charge of trolleys came out and
added some stray ones to the line.

The trolley man had his own names
for most of the regulars.

Hello, Bernie, my old chum!
Greetings, Poodle-oodle-oodle!
And Good Morning to you, too, Specs!

My name is Monty, actually!

The trolley man went away again
and Monty carried on waiting.

Monty eyed the line of trolleys.

'Maybe I could get up into one of
those,' he thought.
So he slipped his collar and had a go.

As soon as he'd settled down, a lady
in a fur coat came along and hauled
Monty's trolley out of the line.

She didn't notice Monty. She
wheeled the trolley inside.

Soon Monty was in the warm, and
there was the sound of soothing
supermarket music.

Monty was sitting in the bottom
part of the trolley — and the lady
was loading tins into the top part.
'She's bought nothing but cat food,'
thought Monty.

They were soon at the check-out counter. The girl at the till began taking tins of Katty-Kit out of the trolley. She didn't notice Monty . . .

. . .until she took out the last tin.

'No dogs allowed in the store!'
she told the fur-coated lady.
'Really!' shrieked the lady.
'Do I look the sort who'd have a
scruffy old mongrel like *that*!'

Just when things were getting
nasty, a man with a moustache
came over and settled the argument.
He seemed to be the manager,
and he took Monty into his office.
Monty prepared himself for a
ticking-off.

But the manager turned out to be friendly. He was in the middle of morning tea, and he gave Monty his slice of fruit cake.

A man of good taste!

Monty was finishing the last mouthful of cake, when the trolley man came in.

The trolley man said that the dog
with the specs had been reported lost
from the Dogs' Waiting Area.
The manager himself took Monty
back to Mrs Sprod. She looked
relieved but embarrassed.

Mrs Sprod fastened Monty's collar.
'Really! Why can't you be patient,
like these other dogs?' she said.
'I've had more fun than *them*,'
thought Monty.